# AL PACINO, the JUDGE

# & I

For all those who have forgotten to smile.

"All the world's a stage...

and one man in his time plays many

parts."

Big Willie S. *As You Like It, Act 11, Scene
V11*

ooOoo

"The world is a stage and the play is badly

cast."

Oscar Wilde. *O'Leary's pub, O'Connell St.,
Dublin.*

ooOoo

"Simply put, the world is staged. Exit

left."

Osgur Breatnach, muttered under his breath.

# CHAPTER 1

## TRAUMA

**Dublin 2010**

'Enough of that!' I said. 'Formally opening our fifth meeting of *The Dublin Book Writer's Club* I welcome you all, although, looking around I see not all of you are here. In more senses than one.'

I eyed the group sat around the table in *O'Leary's* pub in Dublin's O'Connell St. They all looked disturbed. Perhaps the impression came with my knowledge of their past. Not all my invitees had turned up.

'Nevertheless, we have a quorum,' I said. 'So, before I get into my kidnapping did you know that I met him once?'

'Met who?' said Oscar Wilde tuning in to the conversation.

'El Generalissimo Francisco Franco,' I said 'and it was very traumatic. But educational.'

'Pray continue,' said Johnathan Swift.

'I wasn't always the short handsome sixty-year-old man you see before you. Once I was a tanned ten-year-old on a breathless summer's day in Madrid. Hot as only Madrid can be. The sun was high and directly overhead, and the tall street buildings offered no shade.

'The afternoon sun scorched the streets and the intense heat intensified rotten city odors. The concentrated heat suffused my body and bare legs. I walked towards the exciting water fountain in the center of the long *Castellana* street. Eager for the coolness of the forty or so water jets and mist-spray I walked fast. At night they were lit in spectacular colors. But now in the daytime the coordinated shooting sprays and jets caught the sun. They gushed at varying heights towards the cloudless sky like musical notes and formed rainbows. They fascinated me. I walked on and there he was.

'Wielding what looked like a stick he sat on a horse. It was a fine muscular and noble horse.

I wasn't biased against horses. In fact, some of my best friends at the time had similar horses in plastic albeit two inches in height. I admired this artist's fifteen-foot-high bronze work. But Franco, on the other hand, diminutive in contrast, looked silly warding off an invisible threat with a puny weapon.'

'Parece idiota!' I said to my grandmother.

*'Dios mío! No digas eso!'* she implored aghast.

'Of course, as a mischievous child does, I repeated my observation adding further disparaging comments, to her horror.

'Shssssss!' she said, 'Madre de Dios.'

'I desisted only when I realized how terrified she was I would be overheard. Mortified, my

4

granny, *Abuela* as I called her, abandoned the afternoon's excursion and rushed me home to the apartment around the corner.

There, in the shaded coolness of the *piso*'s dining room my *Abuela* explained I must never say anything nasty about Franco. It was dangerous. *Muy peligroso.* I sucked and slurped my way through the sweet slushy *melón* she offered me and nodded contritely to comfort her. Oh, but how I disliked this man! Intensely. A powerful man, that even in the inanimate state of a statue, could terrify my tiny inoffensive *Abuela* twenty years after the Spanish civil war and deny me the cool and beautiful fountain. I was too young to understand the trauma inflicted by the dictator on my mother's family during the aerial bombing of Madrid. Two and a half years before the fall of the city.'

'Hemmingway, when he arrives, can tell us all about that,' said Swift. 'He was there.'

As host, I ordered a round of drinks off the bartender indicating a circle with my finger. Over time,' I continued, 'the more I thought about Franco and our brief meeting, the more I disliked him. In fact, I made it my business to express my dislike of all his ilk as I grew. And as my vocabulary increased, I expressed myself with more eloquence and barbs on fascism and its ideology of fear, loathing and opposition to individualism.

'In the middle of a warm calm night, some twenty years later, when Franco and official fascism were dead, workers arrived with a crane, blow torches and pneumatic drills and carried the sculpture away to some obscure municipal graveyard.'

The face of Brendan Behan appeared in the open window of the snug. I was surprised he turned up for I knew he was barred from the pub.

'Of course, fascist ideology is a fear-response to the traumas of life,' he said.

'We must visit that municipal graveyard,' said Flan O Brien to Myles na Copaleen. 'All those sub-textual conversations between the statues would be worth eavesdropping on.' Then they both tilted back their battered fedoras exposing intelligent brows and balding heads. 'Maybe they should have left a symbolic rider-less horse,' said Behan. 'Sorry I can't come in, but I can give you a Spain and a granny story combined?

'Go on so,' said Wilde

'Long, long ago,' continued Behan, 'and long ago it was, I visited Spain.

'*Is your visit for business or pleasure?*' asked the custom's official.

'I'm here for the funeral,' I said.'

'*A relative?*'

'No, Franco's'

8

'*Franco is not dead!*

'I'll wait,' I said. But they turned me back.'

Laughter.


'That's one of my Spain stories. Now for a Granny one. Once, as a child, when returning home with her and one of her cronies from a drinking session, a passer-by remarked: *'Oh, my! Isn't it terrible ma'am to see such a beautiful child deformed?'*

'*How dare you,*' said my granny. '*He's not deformed, he's just drunk!*'

'Traumatic it was. Being called deformed at such an early age,' he added when the laughter receded.

'Anyway, it was educational for me,' I said,

'but traumatic for my *Abuelita*.'

'Trauma affects us all,' said Flan viewing his

empty pint on the table.

The door opened as the tall thin frame of

James Joyce entered. *And him*, I thought.

'Shite and onions! Hemmingway's not

coming,' he said in disgust. 'He was the same

in Paris!' He put away a small case containing

his ukulele.

*'It sounds too like an Irish affair,'* he mimicked

Hemmingway's American twang. *'Osgur*

*should write and stop talking about it,*

Hemmingway said. I think he just wanted to

go fishing. He took a rowboat up the Great

River that divides our city.'

'Perhaps his curt statement is an indication of one of his famous icebergs,' said Swift.

'Let's hope he doesn't hit one,' said Myles. 'It's freezin' on the river.'

More general laughter.


'So,' said Wilde, brushing dust off his velvet coat, 'to the serious business of the gathering. 'You asked us here to discuss divesting yourself of trauma through writing. Therefore, I offer a modest proposal to the assembly: we should try to undermine our own wit.'

'If, indeed, any should surface,' said Swift looking up at the ceiling and swirling his index finger through the long locks of his shoulder length dark wig.

'I concur, as long as my jar is kept filled,'

added Flan, -'although modest proposals in

Ireland are an extremely difficult thing to find.'

'Can't disagree with that- yet,' said Myles.

Wilde straightened his cravat before saying

'By the way, Myles, I read and enjoyed your

piece in *The Irish Times* on 'modest

proposals'. But I should add, as a wise man

once said, *quotation is a serviceable

substitute for wit,*' and he laughed softly to

himself.

'Brilliant witticism!' said Myles sarcastically,

'he's quoting himself!'


'Eh, coming back to the issue of trauma,' I

continued hurriedly before a row commenced, 'it affects us all at some time in our lives. The memory, and hence the trauma, never goes away but we learn many ways of dealing with it to survive.'

Sage heads nodded, well, sagely.

'Writing is one of my ways. And exposing the farce of denial by a perpetrator is another. In this instance of my story, *Al Pacino, the Judge and I*, I have combined the two.'

'Yes, your present company have all battled and championed for liberty, in and out of court,' agreed Swift.

'I have long battled to save the English language in the Great Court of the Public Domain from the misuse of the apostrophe,' interjected Myles.

'Perhaps trauma is too serious a matter to be dented with either wit or comedy,' warned Wilde.

'Let's be clear,' asked Joyce. 'Is this a true story of yours about either sex, violence, intrigue, betrayal, tragedy, comedy, rebirth, a quest, voyage and return, or overcoming the monster?'

'Yes,' I said, 'all of the aforementioned, but, sadly, without the sex.'

The bartender arrived polishing glasses at the hatch, and eavesdropping, interjected.

'I think every story concerns a trauma if you dig deep enough. Every writer struggles with a physical or psychological trauma and a search for Truth. Now I come to think about it so does every bartender.' Embarrassed at his erudite comments he moved away.

'Well, my story is certainly about both truth and trauma,' I continued. 'You judge if it works.'

'BUT, AS A BACKGROUND to the story,' I continued, 'you need to understand something about our *island in the mist.*'

'Like Hemmingway's *Islands in the Stream*?' said Wilde.

'Tír na nÓg?' said Joyce.

'No! and No!' I said. 'Ireland in the 1970s was in the midst of a mist of trauma. Floating between reality and the figments of many imaginations. Between two worlds.

'For instance, it's years of over-dependence on multinationals saw the result: not the promised fairy tale industrial base but a never forecasted home-made recession.'

'Ah, you changed masters,' said Swift.

'You could say that. Having taken all our generous start-up grants as soon as their five-year tax-free concessions ran out the multinationals said thank you and goodbye. Graciously. They closed their factory doors and left for other more profitable shores,' I continued. 'Our cities, up and down the east and west coasts, and rural areas inland, were all scavenged impartially.'

'I'll accept the accuracy of your words as, not being born yet, I cannot disagree,' said Wilde.

'Why would that ever stop us?' queried Myles, adjusting his battered fedora and clinking his glass with Flann's.

'In my time,' said Swift, 'the same method of engaging investors and politicians, but in a more straightforward and less complicated manner, was availed of – plain bribery, preferably from the taxpayers' purse.'

'So,' I said, 'instead of organising queues of workers *into* factories, government policy switched to organising queues of workers *out of* factories. These closures left hundreds of thousands of workers and their families stunned. But before the subsequent forced mass emigration came the international oil crisis.'

'Ah oil and fire,' said Swift.

'Trauma is far too important a thing ever to talk seriously about,' said Wilde.

I drank a mouthful of Guinness before continuing.

'As you are aware, womanhood has always been considered special in Ireland and treated different than manhood. As writers, women were ignored or banned up to the 60s by the *Office for the Censorship of Evil Literature.* Reading the women's works was illegal. This oversight, or undersight body, went on to ban the work of some 3,000 evil works before they ceased to function, exhausted by the evil they

encountered. Amongst them was our friend

Hemmingway, as he endangered women by

making the earth move around them.

'What's more, not to over-tax women with

responsibility and decision-making, women in

Ireland were refused legal, financial

independence, the right to sit on juries unless

a property owner, refused the right to work in

the civil service if married and refused bodily

integrity, health- the list went on. Indeed, they

were the slaves of slaves.

Some women commented that as they fixed

their hair in their reflections in the glass

ceilings that they noticed the ceilings were

ingrained with barbed wire.'

'It cannot too often be pointed out that women are people,' pointed out Flann.

I shot him a look of acidic rebuke. I had the floor.


'The children of the nation, as per our Constitution,' I continued, shaking my head, 'were given special treatment and attention in churches, industrial schools, orphanages and institutions across the country. Children's dark nights were filled with horrors and not from the effects of bedtimes stories. Indeed, their days weren't much better. But a considerate State and Church shielded us from the more repulsive details- in fact, from all the details.

And there the details lay festering behind

Cannon Law, secret oaths, State

acquiescence and in the shamed frightened

minds of the victims.


'And our educational system was

administered by another country- not England

this time but the Papal State.'

'Individual initiative,' said Joyce, standing up,

leaning on his cane and squinting through his

glasses, 'has been paralyzed by the influence

and admonitions of the church, while the body

has been shackled by policemen, duty officers

and soldiers. No self-respecting person wants

to stay in Ireland. Instead, he will run from it,

as if from a country that has been subjected to

a visitation by an angry Jove. I'm off.'

And with that, donning his boat hat and grabbing his ukulele case, he was gone. Which was just as well, I thought, as you couldn't swing a descriptive noun in the remaining legroom of the smoky sweaty snug. Remember, I had invited them all to the reading on the basis that only one, perhaps two, might turn up. The cost of the alcohol was mounting.

'I've already offered a part solution to poverty,' said Swift. 'Sell poor children to the rich for consumption, thereby enriching the poor while reducing the population explosion, and, collaterally, I might now add, reducing the cost of infrastructure. I have been assured by a very knowing Italian MasterChef late of a BBC culinary program that a young healthy child well nursed is at a year old a most delicious nourishing and wholesome food.'

'I feel so sad and so entirely disappointed that tears are coming into my eyes and a lump of incommunicable poignancy is swelling tragically in my throat,' offered Myles in a lone long sigh.

'Plagiarist!' spat out Flann under his breath, 'I wrote that!'

I continued.

'Citizenship was bestowed on all members of the travelling community, even if second class,' I said, 'to such an extent that our

Minister for Defense, Mr. Donegan, could

shoot at them with a shotgun without any legal

consequences. Such were the times.'

'In our day, politicians had the decency to

shoot themselves in duels,' offered Wilde.

'Or in the foot which they did eloquently in

print or in parliament, or both,' muttered Swift.

'If they were not in parliament, they would not

be given jobs minding mice at a crossroads,'

offered Myles.

I ignored their unhelpful interjections and

continued.

'As the wider community organised in small

groups across the country to defend their

varied rights, our Minister for

Communications, Dr. Conor Cruise O'Brien,

kept a *'remind me'* file of those who

complained in the media's *Letters to the Editor*

pages, presumably for special late night

physical responses by government minions,

when the time was ripe. He was a man who

knew the power of an arrest warrant. After all,

he was an author and a man of letters.'

'Ah how the lessons of history are lost,'

exclaimed Swift!

'Why could they not have used *Noms de*

*Guerre* as I frequently did?

'Yes, well,' I said, 'letters in both my real name

and pen names accumulated in his files.'

Censorship slipped into the national media. Harassment of dissident voices and fear stalked the land. Frightened and overzealous citizens joined in by censoring themselves before the Thought Police pulled them over or knocked at their door. Legal rights were eroded in new legislation, including by the re-introduction of the Special Criminal Court- juryless so as not to inconvenience the citizenry.'

'No juries? Proper order!' exclaimed Flann, 'sure what good is a court of conviction if it can't guarantee to convict everyone before it?

'Up to the forties,' said Myles, 'these special trials were private I recall, short and sweet,

26

presided over by smart articulate army officers. Their memorable judgements echoed deep into the Irish psyche. The prescribed dawn chorus of rifle shots periodically startled the quite of Irish mornings.' The National Bird Watchers Association complained bitterly.'

From the open window of the snug Behan proclaimed a truism.

'It is a little-known fact kept quiet, but nevertheless true, that many judges refuse to sit on this esteemed bench.'

I lit another cigarette.

'I was court martialed by the IRA in my absence once,' said Behan, 'and sentenced to death in my absence, so I said they could shoot me in my absence.'

He broke off to empty his pocket and hand its

contents of coin and notes and a pencil stub

to a passing beggar.

'Ah BB!' said Wilde sadly, 'let me not give

forth on unfair cases,' and he glanced for

comfort at the small patch of blue sky visible

beyond Behan's large head.

'Who in the midst of all our poverty and

distress that threatens to become intensified,'

he continued, 'will step into the breach and

rouse us to the almost superhuman effort that

is necessary to alter the existing state of

things?'

'Hmm, I don't know about the superhuman bit but that's what I and thousands of others did,' I said.

'A problem is that a few millions of our citizens went into denial in fear. Now, that the passing of time has exposed the truth of all that, many are still in denial. The reality exposes their tacit involvement in the suffering of the nation and the prospect of the accompanying guilt is too much to bear.'

The barkeep passed a tray of drinks through the snug hatch and peered suspiciously through the fog of tobacco.

'I hope that Behan fellow is not skulking around in there,' he said, 'remember he's barred!'

He withdrew with a loaded tray of empty glasses.

'Listen!' I said in exasperation at all the interruptions. 'A confusing war raged across Ireland except that it didn't because the Irish government said it wasn't there at all. The war just did not exist. Nevertheless, those who were once alive kept falling over dead due to psychosomatic bombs and bullets. Special political prisons filled with political ghosts.'

'Trauma often results in denial,' said Swift.

'Mind you, up North, a community's requests for esteem, political and legal rights were met with parity. Open aggression, brutality and oppression were dished out to the

complaining community without discrimination

by the British military and British government.

Irish prisons filled to overflowing.

Secret State death squads and *agent*

*provocateurs* worked tirelessly augmenting

the open repression. On a few occasions,

secret British spies publicly bombed Dublin,

not far from where we sit.'

'As Brother Barnabas was want to say,' said

Flan

*'When things go wrong and will not come right*

*Though you do the best you can*

*When life looks black as the hour of night*

*Denial is your only man!'*

and he downed a pint of plain in one gulp.

'Exactly,' I said. 'The Irish government coordinated a policy of *deniability by exclusion* with the British. They excluded the existence of the war. They happily forged a peace policy of talks with inbuilt exclusion. Thereby they excluded a settlement and extended the misery of all- without exclusion of course.'

'Alice in Wonderland! Now you're getting onto our territory,' offered Wilde.

'Yes, such as that of the Irish State to the unreality of Ireland and its economic, social and political reality,' I said.

'Trauma often results in fear,' added Swift nodding.

'There you have it,' I said, animated. 'They reverted to a fear-response. We headed towards the protection of a police state. British

agents lent a hand in the policy of

government, the civil service, the media, the

Irish Army, and the police force.

Daytime police, An Garda Síochána (our

Peace Guardians), were sent forth to contain

potential campaigners at nighttime- before the

would-be demonstrators even got out of bed

and dressed and contemplated

demonstrating.'

'A country must protect itself, particularly

against all invisible enemies,' said Wilde.

'In the case of an invisible enemy any arrests

by the police are a sign of progress,' said

Myles.

The sound of singing came in through the open snug window. A hand was pushed through, and the voice of Behan bellowed. 'I have never seen a situation so dismal' he said 'that a policeman couldn't make it worse. Pass me out a pint of gargle.'

At that moment, a bare-chested body backflipped over the low partition stud wall of the snug and landed languidly laughing. He was so large a man that movement in the snug was now becoming dangerous as accessibility to reach beverages was threatened. From his ornate belt a large salmon hung. He laid his shield and spear on a high shelf.

'Howareyez?' he said. 'I was on a quasi-quixotic quest in search of my son Oisín when I heard of the scintillating storytelling session here by my grandson's namesake. Oisín is the best benefic benign storyteller in Ireland, and I thought he might be here. He went off besotted with a beaded Belarusian blonde on a wingless warmhearted white horse last week and hasn't been seen since. No doubt he'll have a wacky wondrous warriorlike whopper of a tale on his return. Anyone seen him?'

Oscar and Osgur and the rest, none of whom were called Oscar or Osgur, shook their heads.

'Have a drink,' I said. 'It's better than your

usual mead.'

Fionn shrugged his shoulders and continued. 'Apropos invisible enemies you were discussing, my band of Fianna, the finest wardrobed, war-crafted, wandering warriors in the world, often, in most battles and sagas anyway, had to fend off invisible, infamous, ignominious immortal falsehearted foe. Our trauma slips time to this day, no sooner the earth slides to sleep closing its one moon-eye and the sun stretches its warm arms across the stubborn mountains, above birdsong full forests, over rapid rushing rivers and sorcerous faery forts.'

The snug was lulled into silence.

I hurried on in case Fionn was trying to weave one of his magic spells on us.

'Thus,' I continued, 'was birthed in the Ireland of the 'seventies the Garda Heavy Gang. Storytellers *par excellence*. Born tall tale tellers. This was a special squad inaugurated to obtain fairy-tale confessions, by any means, legal or otherwise, from those arrested, innocent or otherwise, true or not.

They even dictated and wrote the confessions out. And kept instructive notebooks on their structure and plot development. The problem was that while the country and continents wrote about and quoted them, the Gang themselves claimed consistently they never existed.'

'Ah, multi-Queens of Hearts in male drag,' commented Myles.

'It was into this zany unreal world that I emerged from my teens. I discovered that war, poverty, failed economic policies; suppression of women, travelers and sexual rights and campaigning groups did not officially exist. All were, apparently, figments of my imagination. And pain was psychosomatic. And society had the bruises to prove it.'

'Attacking imagination is the want of authority,' said Flann, Behan, Wilde, Fionn and Swift in chorus.

'It cannot be too often repeated that Ireland

was bought in 1921 and the transaction was

final and conclusive,' offered Myles.

'Of course, re-sale is another matter,'

muttered Flann.

'Listen, if you continue these interruptions,' I

said forcibly, 'I will stop dead my story. You

are not being helpful. AND there will be no

more alcohol.'

Silence.

OSGUR BREATNACH

# CHAPTER TWO

## SHOW TRIAL

I signaled the barkeep through the hatch and cleared my throat.

'For forty-four years now, I have suffered an ongoing trauma in Ireland. I was kidnapped, tortured and framed for a crime I was wholly and innocent of. Kidnapped thrice, detained eight times in as many days by the Irish police, without access to a solicitor, and subsequently referred to hospital by the High Court.

'I was charged with participation in a train robbery. Tried before a District Court the case against me was thrown out as no evidence whatsoever was produced by the State.

'Subsequently, recharged, tried three times before the Special (non-jury) Criminal Court, in the longest criminal trial in Irish history, I was found guilty and sentenced to 12 years penal servitude.'

'I think it can be assumed,' said Flann 'that they were impressed by your acting performances as they kept asking you to come back for more.'

'Whatever you do,' warned Wilde, 'don't look at their Honors' portraits in their attics.'

'Well, obtaining a pre-ordained result can

sometimes take time,' offered Swift in mitigation, 'and being Chief Justice in Ireland and a vile and profligate villain often go hand in hand.'

'That comment could get me twenty years in the Specials,' I said.

'How so? You never said it. I did,' said Swift.

'Lock up people for making a mockery of justice' asked Wilde? 'Sure, if they did that there would be no judges left to hear cases. They'd be in jail.'

'Another twenty years!' I sighed.

'The law is an ass,' said Behan.

'Or an arse,' said Wilde.

'Or both,' said both Myles and Flann.

'As I said to St. Patrick once, whilst parrying

his encrusted crosier with my swinging sword,' said Fionn shaking his head slowly. 'Our *Brehon Laws*, deemed barbaric and banned, were more reasonable and fairer.'

'The only evidence offered against me,' I continued, 'was a false statement in what a later Appeal Court said I signed under duress and after being oppressed in illegal detention. This evidence followed beatings in a tunnel under the police station and in a police locker room.'

'Ah, the Irish gift of concocting reality from wishful thinking!' said Myles nostalgically.

'The police explained away injuries on my body as being the result of my beating myself up,' I said.

'Now there is imaginative use of the *twist in a tale*,' said Flann admiringly.

The barkeep passed a loaded tray through the hatch.

'The trial court,' I continued, 'when all three judges were awake, declared that one statement was a voluntary admission of guilt, despite my many voluntary statements to the contrary,' I said. 'One judge tended to fall asleep during proceedings. In truth, I was tempted to join him in the vain hope that when I eventually awoke, I would be rid of the nightmare.'

'A-ha, blind AND deaf justice!' said Swift.

'Amnesty International and many other

international groups and individuals across the political and societal spectrum claimed I never got a fair trial,' I said.

'Following an international campaign for my release I won my Appeal 17 months into my sentence and was released, having spent two months in solitary confinement.

The reason the Appeal Court gave for extinguishing my convictions and sentence was that the alleged inculpatory statement was inadmissible due not only to 'oppression' but to unspecified 'other reasons.' Most people, including the *United Nations Declaration of Human Rights*, describe my ill-treatment as physical and mental torture. I

46

was released, the reasoning 'to follow.'

'How is it,' said Swift, 'that the caselaw they quoted for their finding, months later, had not occurred at the time they decided to release you, months earlier?'

'It is clear all is possible down the rabbit hole,' replied Flann, 'and, anyway, justice moves slowly, so slow, it is always overtaken by time.'

'Seventeen years from the date of my first kidnap, after years of stop-and-search harassment, and a civil action for damages taken by me against the State and named Gardaí, the State responded with the wisdom of Solomon and Herod. With no admission of guilt, neither personal nor cumulative, they stopped defending the Gardaí but indemnified them for all their legal costs *ad infinitum.* I grudgingly ended the adversarial negotiations and I received 'compensation.'

There was no acknowledgement of any wrongdoing by the state. 'As a result of my kidnapping, torture and of being framed, and the years in courts and jail and of being harassed, my health has suffered.'

'Jesus don't go to live in Paris!' said Wilde.

'I suffer from Post-traumatic Stress Disorder, what in WW1 was called 'shell shock' and what was renamed in the 1980's as the 'the Vietnam Vets' illness after the war there. Of course, my good name and character and my

earning capacity were and are decimated.

'That I can appreciate,' said Wilde.

'I see doors slam in my face,' I continued.

'Others, I later hear, closed silently before I

ever saw them opening. Far from being

investigated, many of the police involved in

my case were promoted. Both the *Special*

*Criminal Court* and Gardaí have gone on to

perpetrate similar controversial injustices on

others over the years.

'To date the police and the State refuse to

hold an inquiry or a criminal investigation. This

perpetuates my trauma. Every waking day.'

I opened another door silently, the snug hatch,

and signaled the barkeep.

'Hell goes round and round,' indicated Myles with a finger in the air. 'In shape it is circular, and by nature it is interminable, repetitive and nearly unbearable.'

'Laws are like cobwebs, which may catch small flies, but let wasps and hornets break through,' mused Swift.

'That's a great Irish saga,' said Fionn, 'a short story covering a long saga. On the other hand, Oisín's sagas, told over interminable time, cover short spells. Unlike his legendary tales yours are believed less by all Irish persons.'

'Remember' said Flann, 'that I too was Irish. Today I am cured. I am no longer Irish. I am merely a person. I cured myself after many years of suffering.'

'No good deed goes unpunished,' said Wilde sadly looking me in the eye. 'You should write about all that.'

'I have.'

'Well read it out man,' said Wilde, Flann, Fionn, Behan (in through the open window), Myles and Swift in unison.

'OK. But no interruptions!' I demanded, 'until I'm finished.'

'But if you're finished it wouldn't be an interruption,' declared Wilde.

'That's true,' said Myles, nodding his head in unison with Flann.

'Ah lads, come on!'

A comradely silence descended on the snug, except for the satisfying splash of liquid gushing down gullets. Occasionally there was also the resonance of smacking lips.

No doubt in anticipation of my story, I thought.

# CHAPTER THREE

## ART

'My piece is called *Pacino, the Judge and I.* Pacino the actor being he of *Serpico* and of *Salome*, your play Wilde. The judge maintained I was acting in the police station and in court.

He accepted police evidence that I was an accomplished acrobat also as they claimed I had beaten myself up (and there are no stairs to fall down in the middle of a tunnel under the police station.) All this led to my reflecting on theatre, the art of acting and the drama of the story.'

'So here goes *Pacino, the judge and I*.'

'Is it a musical,' asked Brendan?

'No, it's not!'

I cleared my throat.

'Al Pacino, the Judge and I.' I commenced reading.


'I HOPED THE pale October daylight dimming outside the building was not an indication of things to come. The soon-to-be *Chief Justice of Ireland* peered over his glasses at me across the stage of the

courtroom theatre after my marathon

performance.

*'I WAS FRAMED* had been running for almost

a year and making eye contact, the judge said

I was an accomplished actor. I smiled back

gratefully.

'However, obviously unimpressed with the

instinctual lifelong training that developed my

internal sensory, psychological and emotional

abilities (method acting), he went on to

sentence me to 12 years penal servitude.

'To drive home his critical appraisal of the

method acting style, perfected since the

thirties by *James Dean, Marlon Brando, Robert De Niro, Paul Newman* and *Al Pacino,* amongst others, for good measure, he refused me leave to appeal.

'He then instructed the prison warders standing next to me, who I thought were giving me a standing ovation, to take me away.

And so, confirming his promised imminent appointment to the exalted sinecure of Chief Justice, he finally ended the longest running play in Irish history. Or so he thought.

'It's curtains for me,' I commented to the Chorus as I was escorted from the building.

Ireland's Special Criminal Court ensures you get a special trial. Legal and illogical offensive decisions become facts and cannot be appealed. Juries are dispensed with.

'According to Amnesty International the burden of innocence regularly fell to defendants rather than the burden of proof falling to the prosecution. Hidden away in a side street, visitors to this 'open-to-the-public court' faced a gauntlet of armed soldiers and interrogating police.

'Handcuffed to a warder leaving the court I was placed in the rear of the prison van. I bounced up and down as the van drove away.

'This was to remind me that I had been bounced through the legal system in case I needed reminding. We skirted corners behind an advance security detail of armed soldiers, sirens screeching. The detail was replicated to our rear.

'My mind was elsewhere. The muses triggered a new play I began to mentally compose immediately on arrival in jail. After being strip-searched and given a walking tour of the jail I was assured of my safety.

'This is one of the most secure buildings in Europe,' said one prison warder. 'It's a fortified place for free writing. No one will steal your manuscripts here although the Governor might confiscate them, for your own good, like.'

'I was shown the dozen locked and guarded gates between me and any potential threat (critics and the like) outside the 20ft high walls, coils of razor wire and armed guard towers.

That night, as the floodlights periodically blasted the window bars' silhouettes on my cell walls, to drive home the point, they shot a meandering cow (who traversed the no-man's land security perimeter). A kind of welcoming ceremonial slaughter.

'I commenced writing in my cell and launched *Please Release Me Now*, (by inference, a demand for the re-institution of Al Pacino's reputation). The judge's performance, the judge's teachers and their school of acting were being ridiculed internationally by then. In fairness, little did the sentencing judge know of my long-acting career and prowess.

'At the youthful age of nine I had been asked to perform in the internationally renowned Abbey Theatre, which had burnt to the ground the year after I was born and which, I hastily add, had nothing to do with me.

'It was being managed by *Ernest Blythe* at the time of my performance. The part of a leprechaun in *A Christmas Panto* needed to be filled one year and, looking me up and down, he read the introductory letter from my father, then a movie and theatre critic, and asked me to perform.

'From my pocket I pulled out a tin whistle and first played and then sang him a lullaby in Irish. Far from lulling him into a state of somnolence he became agitated.

'We'll call you,' he hastily replied, in English.

'A fascist with a long, checkered background, it has been said that he rejected many good plays in favor of those which were more financially rewarding and that, as a creative force, he consequently ran The Abbey Theatre into the ground. This may explain why the expectant subsequent phone call to me was never made. But then it could have been worse: he could have nominated me for a firing squad, as he did many who offended him during the *Irish Civil War* (an interminable play still running in varied versions for longer than *The Mouse Trap*.)

'I went on to drama school. Unfortunately, I only participated in one class and the lesson should have hinted at any and all future auditions- and many job interviews to boot. I learnt how to close a door quietly behind me. The trick, I can divulge, and which will save you time and a fee, is never to turn your back on the audience. Incidentally, this is generally good practice in life for it is always better to face adversaries than have them sneak up behind you; a chainsaw in the front is much more acceptable than a knife in the back.

'Later, I trod the boards in what I shall call **The Drag Artist** for want of a better name, as its title escaped me then as it does now. A Christmas school-play, it was about something or other which, again, I am now as ignorant of as I was then. It was performed in the late *Gas Company Theatre* in the center of genteel coastal Dun Laoghaire, outside Ireland's capital, Dublin. Suffice it to say that I was volunteered for the part of a woman, dress and wig et all, by the school principal.

63

Leading a donkey to water and all that comes to mind.

'A -la - *Orson Welles*, we gave the audience a hint of a scene and no more than that. Our performance certainly lived up to *Friedrich Schlegel's* theory that good drama must be drastic.

'Probably associated with my ignorance of the play's subject, and indeed my own and the rest of the cast's ignorance of our lines, despite the heavy, loud and prolonged prompting from the wings, clearly audible to the audience but not, unfortunately, to the actors, the curtain never rose after the interval.

'*Arthur Miller* would have approved. By whatever means it is accomplished,' he argued, 'the prime business of any play is to arouse the passions of an audience.' In this case, it did. At my most serious endeavors of pathos audience feelings fluctuated between titters and raucous laughter.

The performance in general was reviewed well enough, if briefly, in the media, despite a subtle hint that the players might have learnt their lines better.

I was 11 years of age and perhaps missed an early lesson in life, one that suggested I should have stuck to comedy in life as perhaps comedy makes a better sense of life's chaos.

'Performing drama in the *Social Street Theatre* I began to be stalked throughout the 70s and 80s, now aged twenty to thirty-something. I accumulated a growing fan base. I even had a performance banned, which is truly a state accolade for any artist.

'Once, on the boards outside Leinster House, the Irish seat of government, despite my voice projection, I could not be heard in the back row of the live event, the wind whisking away my historic, emotive and insightful words ever before they reached the bottom of Molesworth St, or either end of Kildare Street to the front

of the Irish Parliament building. The
performance, like many great Irish artistic
endeavors before it, was technically banned.
This was not because of the performance's
sophistication but because, under *The
Offenses Against the State Act,* all
performances are illegal if held without prior
consent within a half a mile of the national
legislature, either sitting or about to sit, which,
technically, is always.

'Close to a quarter of a million angry,
frustrated and upset people marched
to *Leinster House* in protest at the Irish
government's poor intervention in the *H-Block
Hunger Strike* issue.

'An executive member of the *National H-Block Armagh Group*, it was one of my responsibilities to stay close to the mobile unadorned stage for the drama: a lorry and its sound amplification cargo. Still stalked by some of my aforementioned fans (the *Special Branch*), an interaction in the march behind me distracted me momentarily. I left my position, instructing the driver not to move away from the march and that I would be back in a few moments.

By the time I came back the amplification system and platform had disappeared, the driver threatened by my souvenir- grabbing stalkers.

'Another smaller van and a much weaker

megaphone was located in the swell of the march and pushed to the front that had by now arrived at the gates of parliament. And so, facing a quarter of a million people, my largest audience to date, others and I gave forth to the first three or four human lines of people in a semicircle, the rest of the two hundred and forty-nine thousand seven hundred people having to content themselves with misinterpretations coming down the line.

To this day others reminded me of my historic, emotive and insightful words as I gesticulated artistically, my hair windswept. Chinese whispers being what they are I can confirm regretfully, alas, that I never said them.

'Down the road, such was the reaction, after I performed to a larger crowd at *The British Embassy Gig* that a riot ensued. A section of the audience (the police) ran amok and charged forward looking for me, chasing scores of thousands of the remaining audience all the way to Dublin's city center, a good mile away.

In their determination to get my autograph, my hide, or other keepsake, they chased me first through front gardens, over side walls, and then through back gardens and over more walls, the length of some twenty houses deep, until they gave up while I caught my breath.

'At some duration, some years later, I performed in the Dublin Lord Mayor's home in the full-to-capacity Mansion House Round Room. Here the play *National Birth*, about the establishment of the first government of the new Irish nation, had its first run in 1921 to a mostly armed audience, many of whom marched out in disgust. Audience response can be harsh if insightful.

This time, at the same venue, after giving *The Judge's Performance,* I relaxed as the audiences' hands exited their pockets, empty of guns, to give me a definite emotional response manifested as a standing ovation.

'In *Tailor's Hall*, birthplace of Ireland's longest running play *United Irishmen*, I repeated the performance. It was doubly effective as I gave it bilingually, though not simultaneously, in Irish and English.

'In the nineties, then aged forty something, I returned to street theatre with the Diceman and actor *Mick Lally* (now both deceased) for a photoshoot to promote a fundraiser in The National Concert Hall. Mick Lally's thespian throat loudly heralded the event for a

gathering audience and a TV unit as The

Diceman (*Thom McGinty*) performed one of

his statuesque poses.

'In this case, he was dressed as a dodgy

politician carrying a suitcase full of 'worms,' a

reference to the can of worms that was the

case for which the judge's performance was

being castigated internationally.

'The *Diceman* specialised in standing stock

still in the street, in complete silence,

advertising local businesses and causes close

to his heart.

'Once, when Gardaí asked him to move along,

he frustrated the eviction by employing an

extremely slow-motion walk that, as the

prosecuting Garda told the court, *'was wasting*

*police time as it bordered on immobility, your*

*Honor.'*

'At the interval of the successful National

Concert Hall event, I briefly replaced the MD,

radio impresario *Joe Duffy,* to speak some

lines from *The Judges' Performance*

to applause.


'On another occasion, during a dramatic 're-

enactment,' for publicity purposes, I was being

manhandled by actors dressed as Gardaí.

Film makers and human rights campaigners

*Tiarnan Mac Bride* (now also deceased)

and *Pat Murphy* chose a large institutional-like

building on Molesworth Street, across from

Leinster House, as a backdrop.

'The caretaker appeared in consternation and, matters being explained to him, rather than retreating and leaving the actors to it, immediately proceeded towards the Gardaí. *'Fuck off away!'* he screamed, kicking them repeatedly in the chins.

'This of course turned the theme of the short shoot upside down, inside out. The emotional audience response was not in solidarity with me against my 'arrest' or to facilitate my getaway but because the pillared building was headquarters of, particularly that week, the much maligned, pilloried and publicity-shy *Knights of Columbanus*.

'From acting I progressed to penning *Voices* in co-operation with some of my Special Branch stalkers which was performed in Dublin's *Project Theatre*. It was the classic 'play within a play.' The text was supplied by the police Special Branch, past experts at dialogue.

*'Niall Toibin, Mick Lally (both deceased) and Donal O'Kelly and,* face to audience (mainly media, as it was a PR event publicising the long-running *Release Nicky Kelly* play), read the lines of three detectives. These were given to the trial court performance in which the detectives claimed there had been no collusion, no contact or discussion between them as to any of the content of their

notebooks, purporting their lines to be an independent and uncoordinated true record.

My short play consisted of the actors (pronounced 'actowrs') reading each of the three_statements, alternating paragraph by paragraph between them. *Echoes* was an appropriate title. Of course, all three were practically identical in every respect, including being untruthful. It proved conclusively the mind reading phenomena of the *Dublin Castle's Special Branch Acting School.*

'Years later, following a human rights conference in Dublin, I and many of the participants retired to a local pub to uphold our human right to quench our thirst while rehearsing *Closing Time*. We prepared to leave, the hour being upon us, but in the best tradition of *Waiting for Godot*, we never left.

'The delegation included an exceptionally large number of victims of miscarriage of justices over 20 years in Ireland and England, many of whom are household names such as the *Birmingham Six* and *Guildford Four*. Between us, our past individual and group performances ran for decades, resulting in several hundreds of years' incarceration, (and I suppose I can divulge the twists in the tales at this stage) for crimes we had never committed.

'One minute after *Closing Time* as if by signal, two of my fans arrived led by a Sergeant, all in costume. The sharp sergeant immediately detected the pub was full due to the swell of bodies at the door and adjacent street. Drink was not only still being consumed, brazenly and with style, but was also still being openly sold and he immediately instructed his fellow officers to commence taking names and addresses with a view to prosecution.

'Recognising a true troubadour, he came to me first and I co-operated with the impromptu performance as his foil, as it enfolded, out of respect for a fellow actor- only asking him to

79

deal with me in Irish. He obliged.

'Looking up at the ceiling in solid artistic pose, he gave the impression of trying to recollect where he had heard the name before. Moving on to the persons beside me and all around me he repeated the performance. Within a few minutes he stopped taking details and I could see stage fright taking over as he hesitated.

As well-known name after name was recited to the Sergeant his whirring mind clicked (it could be heard above the late-night din of the pub) and he shook his head as if in a surreal daze, then nodded his head in surrender. *'Why me, why always me,'* I am convinced I heard him mutter.

'Tugging at the sleeves of the other two Gardaí, he led them off stage, (exit left), despite their mutterings and reluctance to abandon a cornered quarry.

'The Sergeant was no fool. It would be farce on the court stage he knew, an unforgettable stigma on his acting reputation, were he to add to the misery of the lives of those he had found quietly supping a late pint.

'It was not lost on him either that representing everyone at any court hearing would be famous stage performer, and fellow late-drinker, international human rights solicitor *Gareth Pierce* who was conversing with me as the Gardaí entered.'

OSGUR BREATNACH

# CHAPTER FOUR

## PACINO'S REPUTATION

'The soon-to-be Chief Justice of Ireland's critique of my method acting, as should be clear by now, was seriously flawed. Far from closing the play down it was a hit and has run now for another 44 years, moving from scene to scene across international stages. It was even positively reviewed by the *United Nations Human Rights Committee*, so much for the judge's judgement.

'He and his panel were wrong not only because they wrongly jailed me for my performance but, of more relevance to our discussion on acting, in that they participated with a troubadour of bad actors in court.

'Detectives changed their lines unflinchingly daily, contradicting their lines delivered at the first trial performance with those given in the second trial performance and those of each other in both performances; all this despite ample loud warning prompts from the bench. Indeed, the performance from *The Bench* itself cannot go unmentioned.

'One of the three judges took off on an

unscripted solo run, tending to nod off during the unimportant matter of witnesses giving forth their best lines and being cross-examined. This was so brilliant a piece of acting that most of the country was convinced he was indeed 'resting' on the bench. This was reasonable as the judges' real performance did not come to the fore until they had to give their pre-scripted guilty judgement at the end of the trial.

'Understandably, the longest performance in Irish legal history, running, as it did then, for almost twelve months, and until the judges came on to perform, as it were, was a bit of a bore for them.

'It took other court extras (clerks) banging doors and deliberately dropping large legal books to wake him from his slumber. When that didn't work, and the presiding judge saw me urgently beckoning my legal team, a swift surreptitious kick under the bench did.

*'The Sleeping Judge* went to the High Court stage whereupon it retreated into an Alice in Wonderland panto stating that the trial court had ruled on itself stating no judge slept and that therefore none had despite any reality to 'the contrary.

'The Broadway-like *Supreme Court of Actors* was more forthright: straightforward condemning our cast for taking the play to

them at all. In a tantrum they threw it off their

stage and into the street *sans* an official

finding.

Thus, we returned to the trial court stage our

unjustified fears allayed, protected under the

unbiased mantle of the Superior Actors.


Shortly thereafter, the ill and medicated

Sleeping Judge slept permanently, and, on his

death, a new trial was ordered.


'That great human rights audience across

Ireland and many across the world disagreed

with all the stage judge's verdicts on my

acting, in fact acclaimed the essence of my

performance, as did later the *Irish Appeal Courts of Criminal Plays*. Eventually. My sentence and conviction were both quashed.

'And so, Al Pacino's method acting style has been reinstated to its rightful place. Seventeen and half years later the Irish government of the day also agreed to cease the historic frustrating and blocking of *My Civil Case for Damages* re-run and bought out all tickets and all future productions and the apparent rights to my play via a substantial compensatory offer.

'The cost was more, it is rumored, than the Birmingham Six ever got for their plays, all of which further attests to the injustice of poor adjudications, or the superior quality of my productions and performances.

'Recently, I have rewritten the play. It's now called *Kidnap, Torture, Framed, Cover-Up* and is due to run nationally and across the continent, and the UN in New York. It includes new scenes based on material uncovered in Government archives from cracks in the floors. It contains such twists as have never been seen since the day St Patrick closed *The Writhering Snake*.

'Like all my plays it simply follows the essence of all good plays, and indeed all art: it simply tells the truth.'

There was a burst of applause in the snug after I finished, and from outside the window. For more alcohol or in appreciation I wasn't sure.

'For the effort,' said late arrival Samuel Becket through the hatch, also clapping. 'But in future fail better.'

Confused, I reached for my Guinness and took a long draught.

'It's himself! We've been waiting for you Becket,' said Behan, his face at the window.

'Comrades, have hope, for everyman, through fear, mugs his aspirations a hundred times a day,' he said.

'Unbelievable!' said Flann O'Brien. 'That story

is obviously plagarised from-'

'-an unpublished Lewis Carol parchment,' said

Myles Na gCopaleen completing the

sentence.

'Imaginative, immoral, impressive,

 international; tearful, tense and timeless in its

seminal scope,' said Fionn Mac Cumhaill,

sucking his Thumb of Knowledge.

'Fantastic!' said Wilde.

'Hey! Easy with the *'fantastic'*,' said Flann.

'They said my last and best book was

fantastic before they rejected publishing it in

the same breath.'

Sadly, Swift said: 'It is a maxim of lawyers,

that whatever hath been done before may

legally be done again; and therefore, they take

special care to record all the decisions

formally made against common justice and

the general reason of mankind.'

'Ok. That's enough quotes for now!' I said.

'Brendan! Lift up that song!'

Behan sang

*'..in the female prison,*

*there are seventy women,*

*I wish it was with them,*

*that I did dwell-'*

-'That's it! screamed the Barkeep in through

the hatch. 'I warned ye Behan was barred.

Get out the lot of you!'

# CHAPTER SIX

## CURTAIN CALL

Outside, we parted in a squall of rain.

From the shelter of the pub's doorway, I

chewed a mint and watched them go.

'Mark Twain and Dorothy Parker promised to

join next week,' I called after them. 'I'll let you

know the venue.'

Flann O'Brian and Myles na gCopaleen ran off

together in the direction of the Irish Times,

accusing each other loudly of having lost the

run of themselves.

Fionn Mac Cumhaill jumped onto the back of a passing stocky thirty-hand-high horse and headed for the hazed hollows of Howth Hill; howling hounds at his heels, his voice cried out into the wind to his son, 'Oisín, oh great storyteller, come home, I have the saga of all sagas for you.'

Joyce had emigrated earlier that day. He got out the better to look in.

Brendan Behan, thrown into a passing police van, feeling quare and banjaxed, settled down with a play he felt coming on. His gentle empathetic soul battled with his fear that

nothing would come of it.

A confused Jonathan Swift kept a firm hand

on his wig as he passed over the nearby

windswept Halfpenny Bridge. Traversing

Dublin's equator North to South in a few fast

yards, it reminded him of a time long past

when he felt lifted by the wind like a gull over

the river. He recalled thinking, man travelling

below the gulls, in the overall scheme of

things, must look diminutive. Gull over

travelling small man. Hmmm.

Back in the present, and amid an identity

crisis, he composed another letter to the

media under yet another pseudonym, which

he mused, could in fact be his real name.

Before also crossing Anna Livia on O'Connell

bridge Oscar Wilde slipped a note into my

hand.

Moving on, he watched the yellow light come

up the quays along the water's edge contrast

with the gold of the rooftops and, in between,

the mass of people suffering in their search for

meaning in poetry, music, prose and art. He

mused loudly to the wind

 '..there is nothing left to say

But this, that love is never lost.'


Upstream, Hemmingway struggled with a

strong Liffey current. The eel of knowledge

swam there it was said. He battled patiently.

Just an old man and a river in a well-lit place.
His fly ran out with the current across the river
and under the bridge. Passing clouds and
diving birds reflected on the water as the light
changed. It was a good light and when a man
has truth in his heart, he knows fish will take
the bait. He tried to interpret the slant of the
line under the surface and all the while he
knew he would not surrender until he caught
one true fish.

Across the city, I perambulated timely, one
step in front of the other. I discovered in an
early life-lesson, that this is the best way to
walk in this world and much less troublesome
than walking backwards or standing still.

Each of us, with our traumas, rushed to the

future. Or, back to the past to our traumas.

Perhaps even both simultaneously.

I opened my hand and read the note Wilde

had given me:

*If you want to tell people the truth,*

*make them laugh, otherwise they'll kill*

*you.*

# ABOUT THE AUTHOR

An award-winning Irish writer in his teens, Osgur Breatnach writes in Irish and English. Over the past fifty years, he has worked as a human rights activist, business consultant, journalist, publicist, lecturer, cartoonist, contributor, and advisor to controversial TV documentaries and two Irish best sellers. He now writes novels, movie treatments and scripts, poetry, short stories and is completing a memoir.

www.osgurbreatnach.com

# By the same author

**Non- fiction**

*A State Conspiracy*
*Framed through the*
*Special Criminal Court-*
*The 'Great Train*
*Robbery' trial* (with
Mary Reid).
*Irlande J'acuse*
*The Sallins Case Exposed*

**Poetry**

*Hanging Out on the 11th*
*Floor*
*The Pregnant Man*
*Winter in captivity*
*Last Words.*

**Novels**

*Deathly Secrets*
*Out of the Tunnel*
*Thief*
*Frontline*

**Short Fiction**

*Al Pacino the Judge & I*

*The Second Death of*
*Octavius Murphy*

**Short story collections**

*TellTale*

*War Stories*

**Journalism**
**Editor/writer/designer:**

*Local News * Local*
*Voice * Hibernia **
*Sunday World*
* *The United Irishman **
*Development * Sunday*
*Press * Irish Press **
*Evening Press * Evening*
*Herald*
* *Irish Independent **
*Sunday Independent*
* *The Starry Plough.*

**Public Relations**

*National Secondary Student's Union * National Housing Action Groups * National H-Block Armagh Committee * Release Nicky Kelly campaign * Sallins Inquiry Now campaign * Image Innovative Solutions*

**Plays**

*Voices*

**Researcher/ Contributor**

*Blind Justice*

*Round Up the Usual Suspects*

**TV & Radio (Story/
Interview/ Contributor/
Researcher):**

*Frontline* RTE

*Open Those Gates*
Channel4

*The Gay Byrne Show*
RTE1

*Scandal/Scannal* TV

*Finné/Witness* TG4

*Night Hawks* RTE1

*Though the Heavens May
Fall* RTE1

*At the Hands of the State/
Faoi Lámh an Stáit* TG4

*The Whistle Blower*
RTE1

**Podcasts**

*The Policed* (1) with
Vicky Conway

*The Policed* (1) with
Vicky Conway

*Osgur Breatnach & the
Sallins Inquiry* with Mick
Clifford Irish Examiner.

**Movie Treatments &
Scripts:**
*Deathly Secrets*
*Out of the Tunnel*
*Thief*
*Frontline.*

**Awards**
Winner national short
story competition *Inniu*
newspaper
Scolarship to University
College Dublin
Best seller *Blind Justice*
Best seller *Round Up the
Usual Suspects*
Jacobs TV Award
*Though the Heavens May
Fall,*

Award-winning *At the Hands of the State/ Faoi Lámh an Stáit.*

**Awards-winning The Whistle Blower:**
*Most listened to RTE *DocOnOne* (2019)
*Most listened to RTE homegrown programme (2019)
*Law Society Justice Media Award (2020)
  ***New York Festivals International TV & Film Radio Award** (2020)

First published in Ireland

in 2020 by

Plus**Art**online.

First published on Kindle in 2020 by

Plus**Art**Online.

10 Highthorn Park,

Mountown, Dun Laoghaire,

Co. Dublin. Ireland.

admin@ PlusArtOnline.com

Typeset by Pink Banana Web Ltd.

Design by Saoirse Breatnach.


Special thanks to Myles and the lads.

Great craic.

Printed in Great Britain
by Amazon

17834136R00068